Y0-EKA-284

VAN BUREN PUBLIC LIBRARY
118047 NBA Finals, The

# NBA FINALS

Published by Creative Education, Inc.
123 South Broad Street, Mankato, MN 56001

Designed by Rita Marshall with the help of Thomas Lawton
Cover illustration by Rob Day, Lance Hidy Associates

Copyright © 1990 by Creative Education, Inc.
All rights reserved. No part of this book may be reproduced in
any form without written permission from the publisher.

Photography by Allsport, Duomo, Focus on Sports,
Photri and UPI/Bettman Newsphotos

Printed in the United States

Library of Congress Cataloging-in-Publication Data

Stevenson, Amy
　The NBA Finals/by Amy Stevenson.
　　p.　cm.
　Summary: Discusses the history of the NBA Finals champions, including players, exciting games and dominant teams from the league inception in 1949 to the present.
　ISBN 0-88682-314-5
　1. National Basketball Association—History. 2. Basketball—Tournaments—United States—History. I. Title.
II. Title: National Basketball Association finals.
GV885.515.N37G66　1990　　　　　　　90-30975
796.323'6—dc20　　　　　　　　　　　　　CIP
　　　　　　　　　　　　　　　　　　　　　AC

# NBA FINALS

AMY STEVENSON

CREATIVE EDUCATION INC.

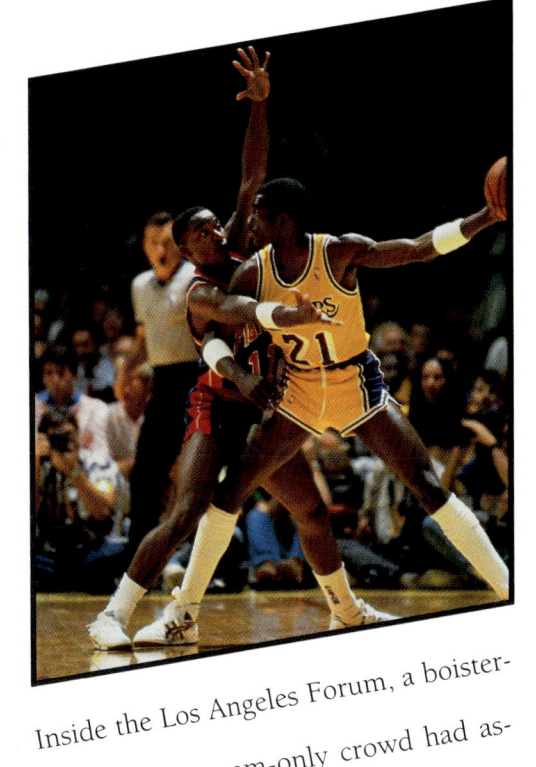

Inside the Los Angeles Forum, a boisterous, standing-room-only crowd had assembled to witness the final game of the 1988 National Basketball Association championship. The battle was between the league's two best—and most diverse—teams: the Los Angeles Lakers and the Detroit Pistons.

The Lakers, who featured a torrid fast break, were seeking their second straight league championship, a feat that had not been accomplished since 1969. In contrast, the Pistons, looking for their first-ever NBA title, had fought their way to the top of the league behind their formidable defense.

With the series tied at three games apiece, the Lakers had seemingly taken control of game seven. Their victory appeared to be inevitable, until Detroit engineered a 17–4 run late in the fourth period. Now, with only six seconds remaining in the game, the Lakers held a fragile one-point lead.

All eyes in the arena focused on Laker James Worthy as he received the inbound pass. While Worthy tried to find an open man, the menacing Piston defense drew closer. The championship hung in the balance. After seven grueling months, the season came down to this one great moment.

*The Detroit defense surrounds Kareem Abdul-Jabbar.*

## THE MIGHTY MIKAN

The history of the NBA Finals is filled with thrilling moments provided by talented teams such as Detroit and Los Angeles. Dynasties have been forged, superstars have emerged, and rivalries have flourished as the NBA's best vie for the league title.

*James Worthy must shoot, or find an open man to pass the ball to.*

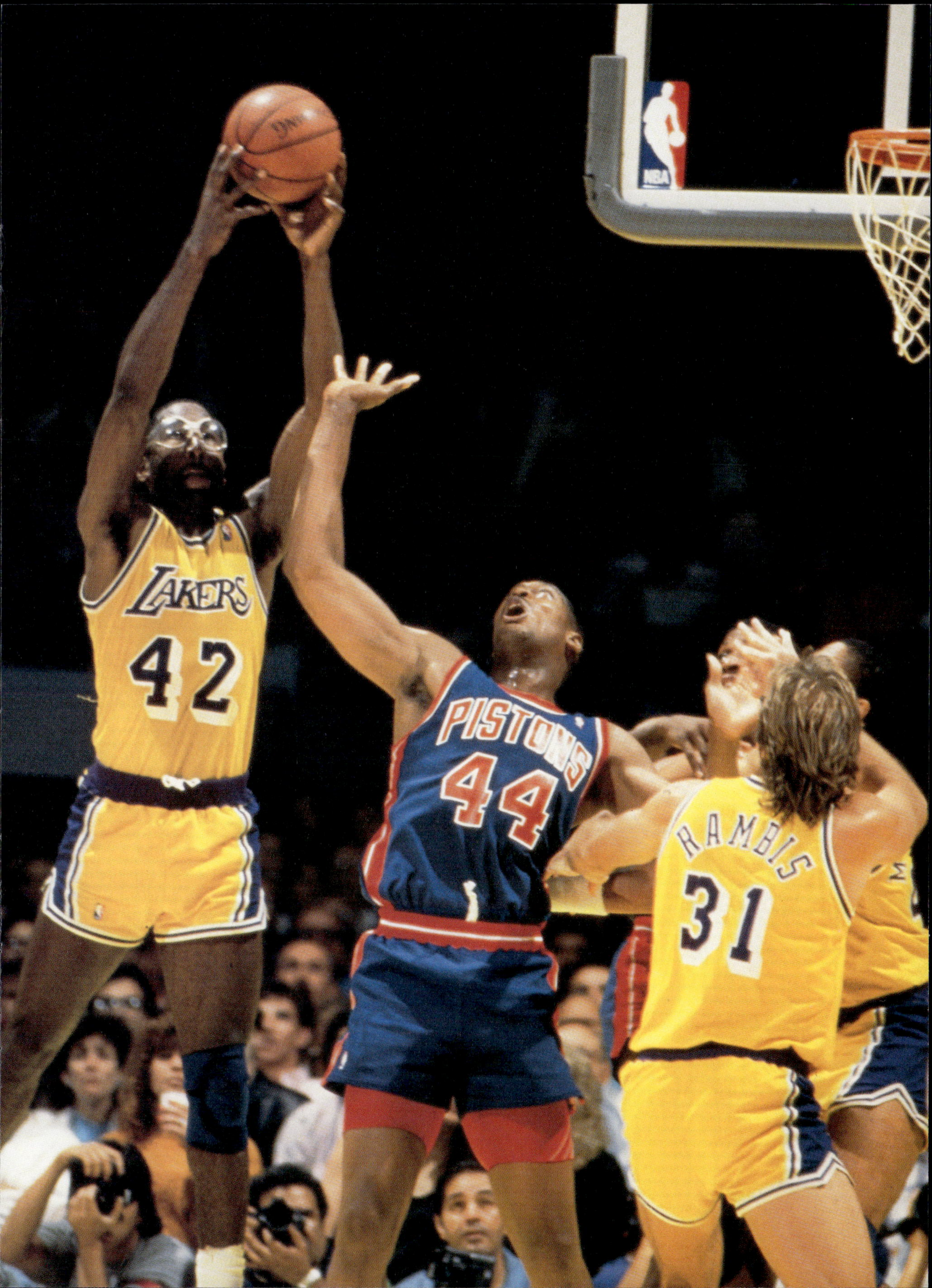
LAKERS
42
PISTONS
44
RAMBIS
31

The NBA tradition of exciting moments began back in 1949. That was the year that two rival professional leagues, the National Basketball League and the Basketball Association of America, merged to form the NBA.

At that time, professional basketball held little resemblance to the game that is played today. Teams would rarely score more than seventy or eighty points a game. Dunks, three-point baskets, and seven-foot centers were nonexistent.

The nature of the game began to change when the first NBA Finals was won by the Lakers, who played in Minneapolis at that time.

The Lakers' leader was a six-foot-ten giant named George Mikan. The three-time All-America from DePaul University dominated league scoring, becoming the first player to reach the ten thousand-point mark. Until this time, it was thought that players over six foot six would be too clumsy to play professional basketball. Mikan proved all the critics wrong.

*Basketball has become a fast, high-scoring and physical game, since the first NBA Finals in 1949.*

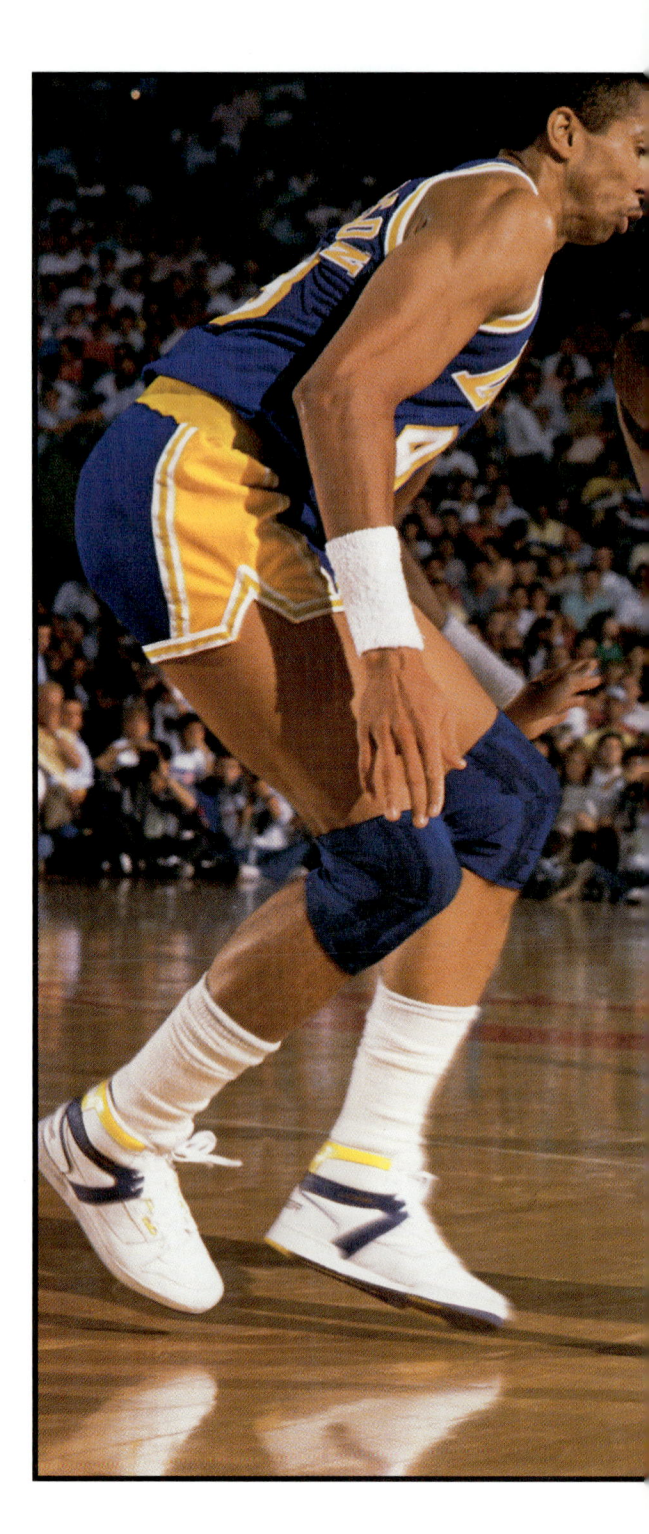

*Number 99 George Mikan of the Minnesota Lakers.*

His specialty was a pivot shot that opponents found nearly impossible to combat. Although Mikan's awesome scoring provided most of the team's offense, the Lakers had a balanced attack and had another talented scorer in forward Jim Pollard.

Their opponent in the 1949 Finals was a team called the Washington Capitals, coached by a fellow named Red Auerbach. Auerbach would soon become the coach of the Boston Celtics and, eventually, the most successful coach of all time. But his Capitals were no match for Mikan and the Lakers.

Washington knew Mikan would be a challenge to stop. During the play-offs, he had averaged more than thirty points per game. When he continued to dominate play during the Finals, the Capitals were forced to key their defense on him. Although they held Mikan to a mere ten points in game two, the rest of the Lakers poured in enough points for an easy victory.

During the fourth game of the series, Mikan broke his wrist. An injury like this would sideline any other player. But Mikan was an extraordinary athlete with a powerful will to win. Playing with a cast on his arm, George led the Lakers to a 77–56 rout before ten thousand screaming hometown fans to capture the team's first championship. It was the first of many moments in the history of the NBA Finals.

*Like George Mikan's pivot shot, Kareem's "Sky Hook" was difficult to block.*

## THE CELTIC DYNASTY

Throughout the years, there have been numerous league champions, but few teams have given basketball fans more thrilling moments to remember than the Boston Celtics. While the Lakers were winning the first NBA Final, the Celtics had languished at the bottom of the league. But owner Walter Brown was determined to make Boston a winner. At the time, no one had any idea of how wildly successful Brown would be. His first move was to hire a new coach. The man he selected, Red Auerbach, was then unknown but would soon become a legend for his mastery of the game. A colorful man known for his excitable nature, Auerbach was also a gifted teacher who could often bring out players' hidden talents.

But even Auerbach was skeptical when Bob Cousy's name was picked out of a hat during a college draft by Walter Brown. Red had already bypassed Cousy earlier in the draft. Even though Cousy was an All-America and the number one scorer in Holy Cross history, Auerbach thought the six-foot-one guard was just too small to play professional basketball.

Cousy quickly made a believer out of Auerbach, the Celtics, and the rest of the league. Bob became the team leader and a playmaker of the highest order. He dazzled his opponents with his deft ball handling skills and was soon nicknamed the "Mighty Midget." After a spectacular rookie season, Cousy was named rookie of the year in 1951. Clearly, he belonged in the NBA.

*Bob Cousy weaves between Detroit defenders and lays up another two points.*

While Cousy alone vastly improved the ball club, it wasn't until Bill Russell joined the team in 1956 that they became a championship contender. Russell, a powerful rebounder and shot blocker, had been a star at the University of San Francisco, where he had led his team to two consecutive National College Athletic Association championships.

Once in the NBA, Russell continued to dazzle opponents with his amazing talents. According to Auerbach, Russell could play a whole team defensively. "He could get anything within fifteen feet of the basket, blocking as many as four separate shots on one play," Red said. "Because of Bill Russell, defense became an important part of basketball."

With the addition of Russell—plus another rookie, high-scoring Tommy Heinsohn—the Celtics advanced to the NBA Finals in 1957. Their opponents, the St. Louis Hawks, were heavily favored to win the series. Yet the championship evolved into one of the most spectacular seven-game series in the history of the NBA.

*Tommy Heinsohn (15) helped the Celtics get to the 1957 Finals—his rookie year.*

*Bill Russell (6) and Wilt Chamberlain (13)*

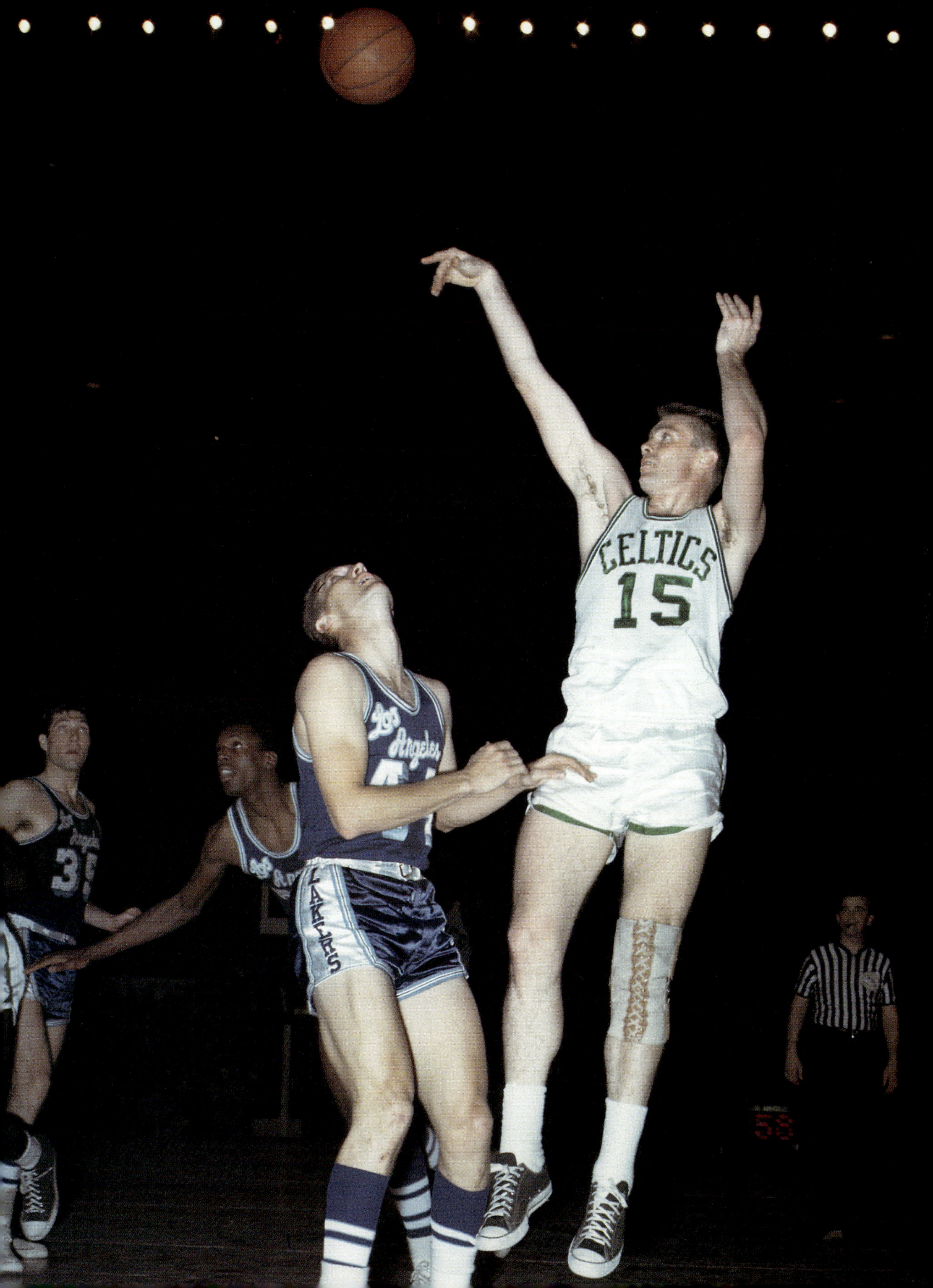
CELTICS
15
Los Angeles
LAKERS

The Hawks won the first game in double overtime. The Celtics evened the series by winning the second game easily. St. Louis responded by winning the third contest by a basket. To everyone's surprise, Boston bounced back to win the next two games. Suddenly, Boston was one victory away from winning their first NBA Final. The Celtics hoped for an easy win in game six, but St. Louis had other plans. The game was tied with only twelve seconds remaining when Bob Cousy was fouled. All he would have to do is drop one free throw and Boston would win the championship. Normally, this would be an easy point for Cousy, but this time he missed. St. Louis grabbed the rebound and hurried the ball downcourt. Cliff Hagan received the ball under the Hawks' basket. Surrounded by Celtic defenders, Hagan managed to put up a shot with only one second left in the game. Miraculously, the ball sailed through the basket; St. Louis had tied the series at three games each.

*With only one second left, St. Louis won Game Six of the 1957 Finals.*

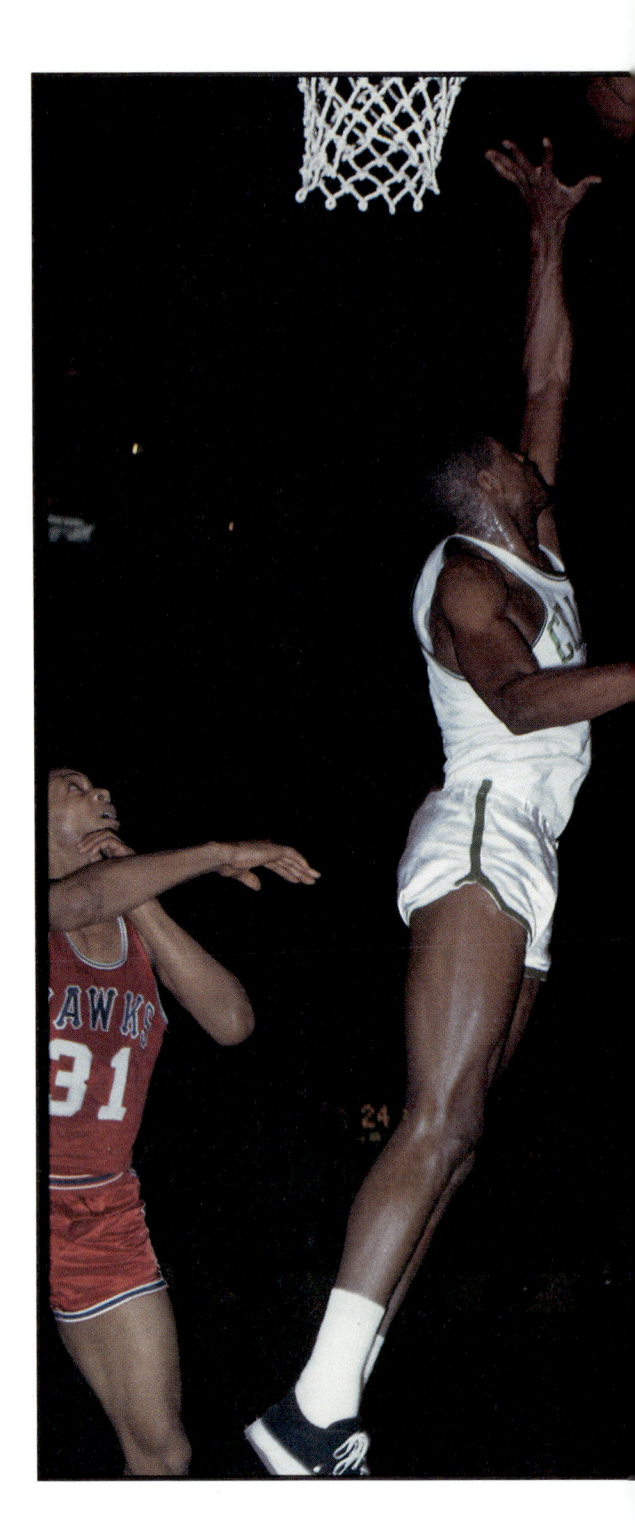

The season now came down to a single game in the Boston Garden. For perhaps the first time in the history of the NBA, the nation's attention was focused on the sport. Basketball fans across the country eagerly awaited the final contest.

*Bill Russell (6) puts up a hook shot over St. Louis Hawk Clyde Lovellette (34).*

They would not be disappointed. Game seven became an instant classic. The score was tied twenty-eight times, and the lead switched thirty-eight times, as both teams battled for the championship. The game went into double overtime, with the teams still deadlocked. With two seconds remaining, Jim Luscutoff dropped a free throw, putting the Celtics two points ahead. The Boston fans were certain that St. Louis wouldn't have time to get off another shot.

But Alex Hannum, the Hawks' player-coach, set up one last play. Before he passed the ball in bounds, Hannum positioned Hawks' star Bob Pettit directly under the St. Louis basket. Hannum threw a court-long pass that bounced off the Hawks' backboard. Russell and Pettit fought for the rebound. Pettit managed to wrestle the ball away and threw up a shot as the buzzer sounded. All night, Pettit's shots had been amazingly accurate. Ironically, this easy shot touched the rim of the basket . . . and dropped off. For a moment, the Celtics and their fans were stunned. Then the celebration began. The Boston Celtics had won their first NBA Final!

That victory was just the first of many great moments the Celtics would provide basketball fans throughout the next few decades. During the 1950s and 1960s, the team built a basketball dynasty. Over a thirteen-year span, the Celtics won eleven titles, including a phenomenal eight straight championships.

It was the teamwork of Cousy, Russell, Heinsohn—and later, John Havli-

*Kevin McHale of today's Celtics battles underneath with hopes of advancing to the Finals.*

cek—that brought championship after championship to Boston. The game of basketball is by its very nature a team game. A great team needs talented players who can shoot, pass, rebound, and defend well. No one player can ever win the NBA title on his efforts alone. However, there have been occasions in the history of the league where an entire team has been inspired to victory because of the actions of a single player.

## A LEADER'S COURAGE

The 1970 NBA Final is an example of such a great moment. The contest featured the Los Angeles Lakers versus the New York Knickerbockers. The Laker lineup boasted some of the league's best players, including Wilt Chamberlain, Elgin Baylor, and Jerry West, all future Hall-of-Famers. In contrast, the key to the Knicks' success was the perfect balance between their well-crafted offense and defense. Captained by Willis Reed, the Knicks had many hardworking players like Bill Bradley, Walt Frazier, and Dave DeBusschere.

The series began in New York, where the teams split the first two games. The battle heated up in Los Angeles, where the next two games went into overtime, with each team gaining another victory. The series remained tied, now at two games apiece.

*John Havlicek (17) contributed to the Celtic's success throughout the 60's.*

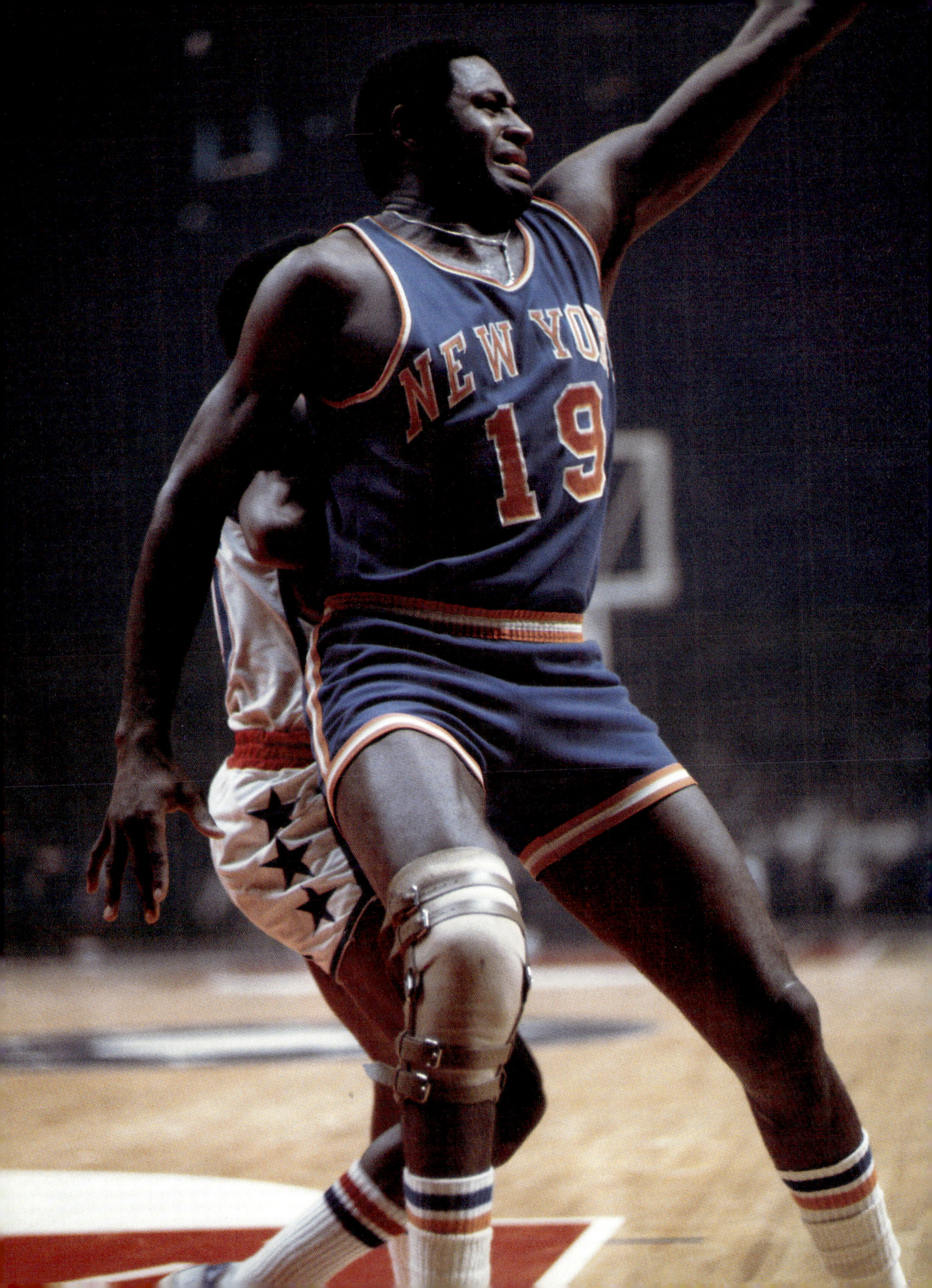
NEW YORK
19

Then, during the fifth game, tragedy struck the Knicks. As Willis Reed drove to the basket to defend Chamberlain, he suddenly crumpled to the floor. Reed, New York's defensive leader and top scorer, had torn a muscle in his thigh. He lay helpless on the court, grimacing in pain. The nearly twenty thousand spectators in attendance at Madison Square Garden let out a gasp in unison. After being helped to his feet, Reed insisted that he continue playing. But soon the pain became unbearable, and he had to be helped to the sidelines. To everyone in the Garden and the millions of fans watching the game on television, it appeared certain that Willis Reed was finished playing basketball for the season.

The Knicks pulled together and somehow managed to win game five. But Reed's absence was clearly evident in the next contest. Without him, the Knicks simply could not stop Chamberlain. The Lakers coasted to an easy victory, with Wilt stuffing in forty-five points and grabbing twenty-seven rebounds. It looked as though Los Angeles was certain to capture the title in the final game.

Then one of the greatest moments in basketball history took place. A few minutes before game seven began, Willis Reed limped onto the court, dragging his injured leg. His teammates and the Lakers, nearly finished with their pregame warm-ups, stared at him in amazement. The stunned crowd in Madison Square Garden gave Reed a standing ovation. The cheers and applause continued and grew louder as Willis walked onto the court to take his place in the starting lineup.

*Willis Reed of the New York Knickerbockers.*

*Hall-of-Famer Wilt Chamberlain.*

*Lakers and Pistons during the 1989 Finals.*

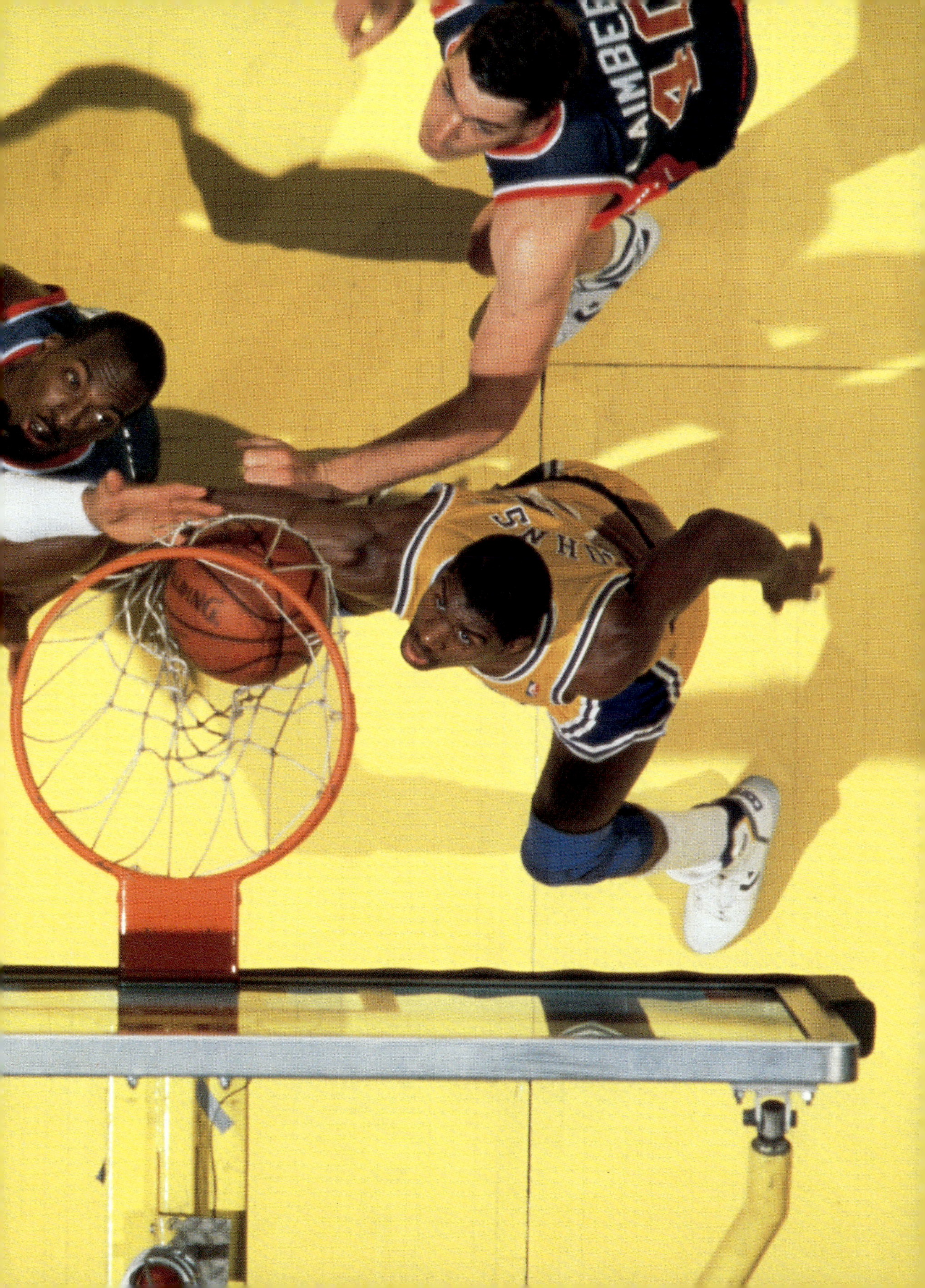

The game began with Los Angeles winning the opening tip-off, but the Lakers couldn't score. The Knicks rushed the ball downcourt to Reed, who scored a basket with his very first shot. A few minutes later, Reed sank another jumper even though he was limping badly. Willis didn't score another point that night, but he didn't need to. Inspired by their captain's courage, the Knicks quickly took control of the game. By halftime, they had built a twenty-seven-point lead; after that, the end result was never in doubt. When the final buzzer sounded, the entire Garden went wild. The Knicks had won their first NBA championship, thanks in part to the unselfish leadership of Willis Reed.

## MAGIC AND BIRD

Throughout the history of the NBA, there have been a few special players, like Willis Reed, who could directly influence the final outcome of a game by their mere presence in the starting lineup. But there have been far fewer individuals who have made an impact not only on their own ball club but on the entire league as well—players who have led their teams to one NBA championship after another.

No two players fit this description better than Earvin ("Magic") Johnson and Larry Bird. During the 1980s, these two players and their teams dominated the NBA in a way that few had before. Throughout the decade, not a single NBA Final was played without either Bird or Magic. Johnson led the Los Angeles Lakers to five NBA titles during that time, while Bird and the Boston Celtics collected three championship rings.

Bird and Magic both joined the league in 1979, fresh from their meeting at the NCAA finals, where Magic's Michigan State team defeated Bird's Indiana State team for the college championship.

*While Larry Bird was named Rookie-of-the-Year in 1979, Magic Johnson played all the way to the NBA Finals as a rookie.*

Both players made an immediate impact on their teams. Bird was named rookie of the year and helped the Celtics post a thirty-two-game improvement over the previous season. Meanwhile, Magic and his teammates had a stellar 60–22 record and found themselves in the NBA Finals.

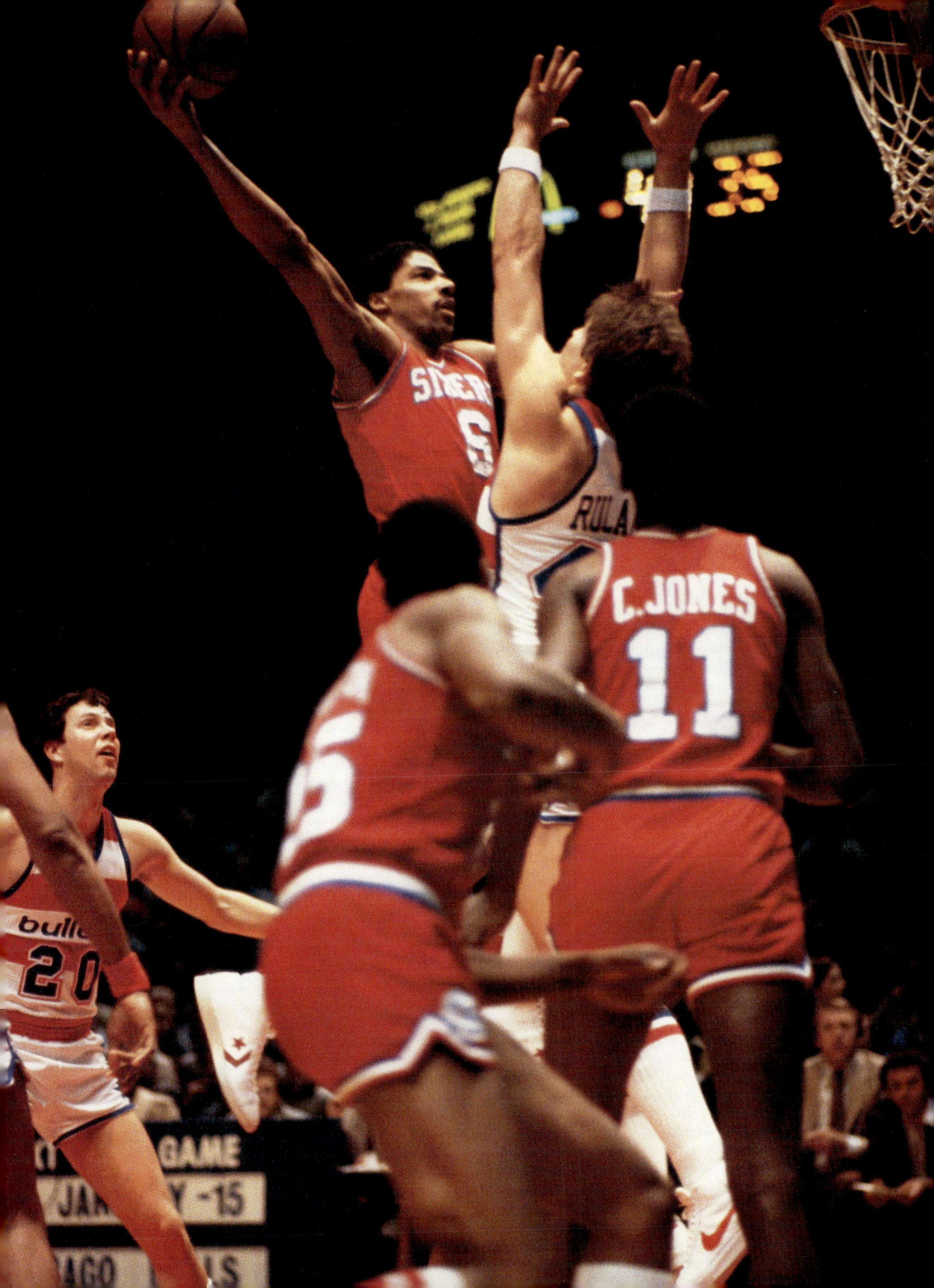

SIXERS
6
RULA
C.JONES
11
bulle
20
GAME
JAN Y -15

The Lakers' opponents were the powerful Philadelphia 76ers, led by their star forward Julius Erving. The teams were evenly matched, which became evident as the teams split the first four games of the series. In game five, the Lakers swept to victory behind the brilliant play of Kareem Abdul-Jabbar. Now Los Angeles was just a victory away from the NBA championship.

However, a crisis loomed. Jabbar had twisted his ankle severely during game five and wouldn't be able to play during the rest of the series. How could coach Paul Westhead replace his legendary center? He decided to gamble on rookie Magic Johnson, the point guard who hadn't played center since high school.

Magic rose to the challenge. In game six, he scored forty-two points, grabbed fifteen rebounds, and made seven assists. Los Angeles had won the title once again, and Magic was the first rookie ever named most valuable player in the championship series. It was another great moment in the history of the NBA Finals.

*Julius "Dr. J" Erving led the Philadelphia 76ers to the NBA title in 1983.*

While Larry Bird's contributions to the Celtics' championships were not always this dramatic, he was just as instrumental to their success.

"The Boston Celtics don't win without Bird, and the Los Angeles Lakers don't win without Earvin," said Laker coach Pat Riley. "They don't. I mean, they win games, but they don't win championships. There's a difference."

*Los Angeles Lakers coach Pat Riley.*

During the course of the 1980s, their teams battled each other for the NBA championship three times. When the teams met in the Finals in 1984 and 1985, the Celtics and Lakers were clearly the top clubs in the league. Both series went the full seven games and were decided by slim margins, with Boston winning in 1984 and Los Angeles victorious the next year.

They met again in the 1987 Finals, with Boston attempting to repeat as league champs. However, the Lakers had plans of their own. They quickly built a 2–1 game lead in the series. Although game four proved to be the turning point in the series for the winners, the spectacular ending was exciting for both team's fans. With less than a minute remaining in the game, the Celtics were up by a point. Suddenly, Magic found Jabbar all alone under the Laker basket and fired him a rocket pass that led to an easy basket and a one-point Laker lead. The Celtics responded immediately. Bird grabbed the ball and raced downcourt. With only twelve seconds remaining, he launched a three-point field goal attempt. The ball swished through the basket.

*Larry Bird attempts a three point shot.*

But the Lakers weren't finished. Jabbar was fouled and took his place at the free throw line. His first shot spun off his fingertips and dropped through the hoop. The second shot went off the rim but bounced off one of the Celtics before going out of bounds. Now the Lakers, down by one point, had the ball and a chance to win the game. Only four seconds remained.

*Jabbar from the free-throw line.*

Magic received the inbound pass. He looked to pass, but all his teammates were covered. So he began to set up for a jump shot. Suddenly, three Celtic defenders jumped out at him. Time was running out; Magic had to think quickly. He pivoted and took a running hook shot from near the foul line. The ball arched perfectly and sailed through the basket for another thrilling Laker victory and a commanding lead in the series.

Although the Lakers went on to win the title, few fans doubt that Magic and Bird will meet again in the NBA Finals someday. Throughout the years, the two players developed a friendly, professional rivalry that served only to enhance their performances.

"We both have made each other better players," Johnson said. "I think we push each other, and we push each other to stay not only at the top of our game, but also to make our teams stay at the top. We both play the same type of game. We're both out there to win, and we'll do anything to win."

*Magic Johnson looks to pass.*

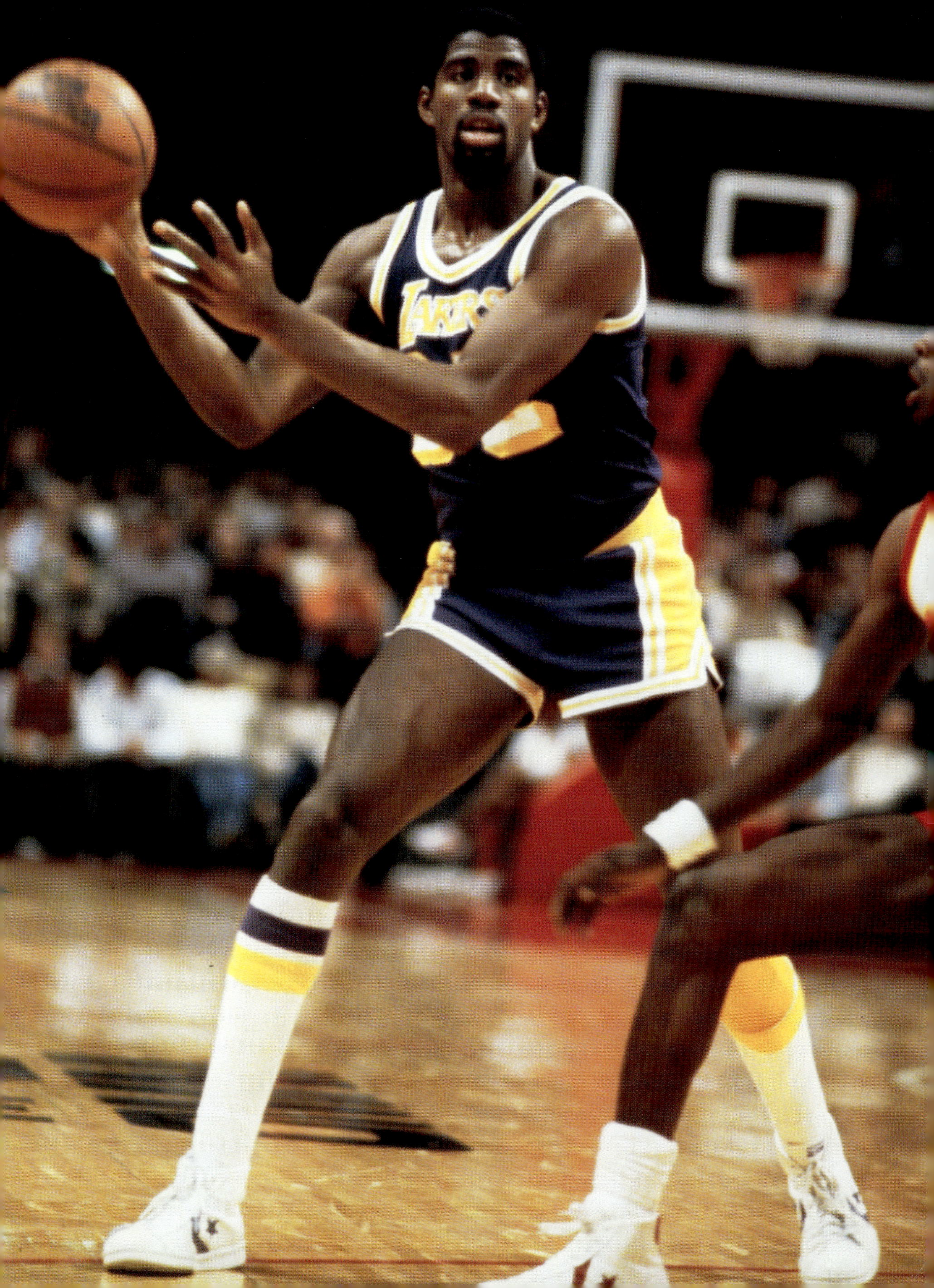
LAKERS

It was a feeling of mutual respect that Larry Bird shared. "If we don't win, I always want to see him win," he said. "It's a funny thing. But I also want to catch him," Bird added.

Players like Magic Johnson and Larry Bird, and teams with the storied traditions of the Boston Celtics and Los Angeles Lakers have helped make the NBA Finals one of the most thrilling spectacles in sports since its beginnings in 1949.

Basketball fans throughout the world were treated to another exciting series in 1988. The veteran Los Angeles Lakers were seeking to repeat as NBA champions, but they were being severely tested by their young, aggressive opponents, the Detroit Pistons.

Each team had won three of the first six games of the series; the winner of the final contest would become champions of the NBA. All of the practice shots, scrimmages, free throws, rebounds, and field goals of the past year had led these two teams to this climactic moment.

Isiah Thomas (11) of the Detroit Pistons sets up a play during the 1988 Finals.

With a mere six seconds remaining in the contest, the Lakers were trying to protect their slim one-point lead. James Worthy looks to pass. One more field goal would give the Lakers a commanding lead, but if the Pistons manage to come up with the ball, they could easily win the championship.

*A. C. Green scores two points for the Lakers.*

Quickly, Worthy threads a pass through the Piston defense to teammate A. C. Green. Green grabs the ball and works his way toward the Laker basket. As the seconds tick away, Green puts up a shot, knowing it is quite possibly the last chance the Lakers have to score this year. As the ball spins through the air, the crowd roars in anticipation of victory. Jubilation fills the arena as the ball sails through the basket.

The Los Angeles Lakers have won the championship and written one more chapter in the history of the NBA Finals, giving basketball fans another great moment to remember.